First PEAS to the Table

How Thomas Jefferson Inspired a School Garden

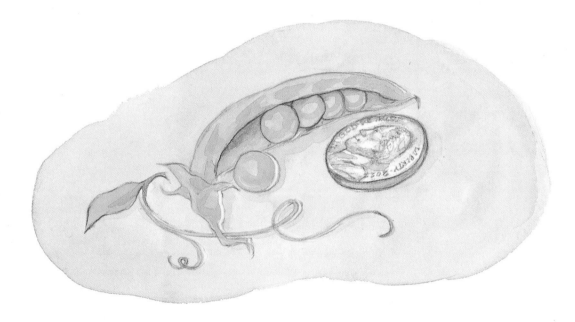

Susan Grigsby   Illustrated by **Nicole Tadgell**

www.av2books.com

Your AV² Media Enhanced book gives you a fiction readalong online. Log on to www.av2books.com and enter the unique book code from this page to use your readalong.

AV² Readalong Navigation

HIGHLIGHTED TEXT

HOME ⌂

CLOSE ⊗

START READING

READ

TITLE INFORMATION

INFO

READALONG BACK READ NEXT INFO

PAGE TURNING

BACK NEXT

PAGE PREVIEW

Go to **www.av2books.com**, and enter this book's unique code.

BOOK CODE

L45828

AV² by Weigl brings you media enhanced books that support active learning.

First Published by

ALBERT WHITMAN & COMPANY
Publishing children's books since 1919

Published by AV² by Weigl
350 5th Avenue, 59th Floor New York, NY 10118
Website: www.av2books.com   www.weigl.com

Printed in the United States of America in North Mankato, Minnesota
1 2 3 4 5 6 7 8 9 0   17 16 15 14 13

052013
WEP250413

Library of Congress Control Number: 2013908333

ISBN 978-1-62127-876-4 (hardcover)
ISBN 978-1-48961-431-5 (single-user eBook)
ISBN 978-1-48961-432-2 (multi-user eBook)

Text copyright ©2012 by Susan Grigsby.
Illustrations copyright ©2012 by Nicole Tadgell.
Published in 2012 by Albert Whitman & Company.

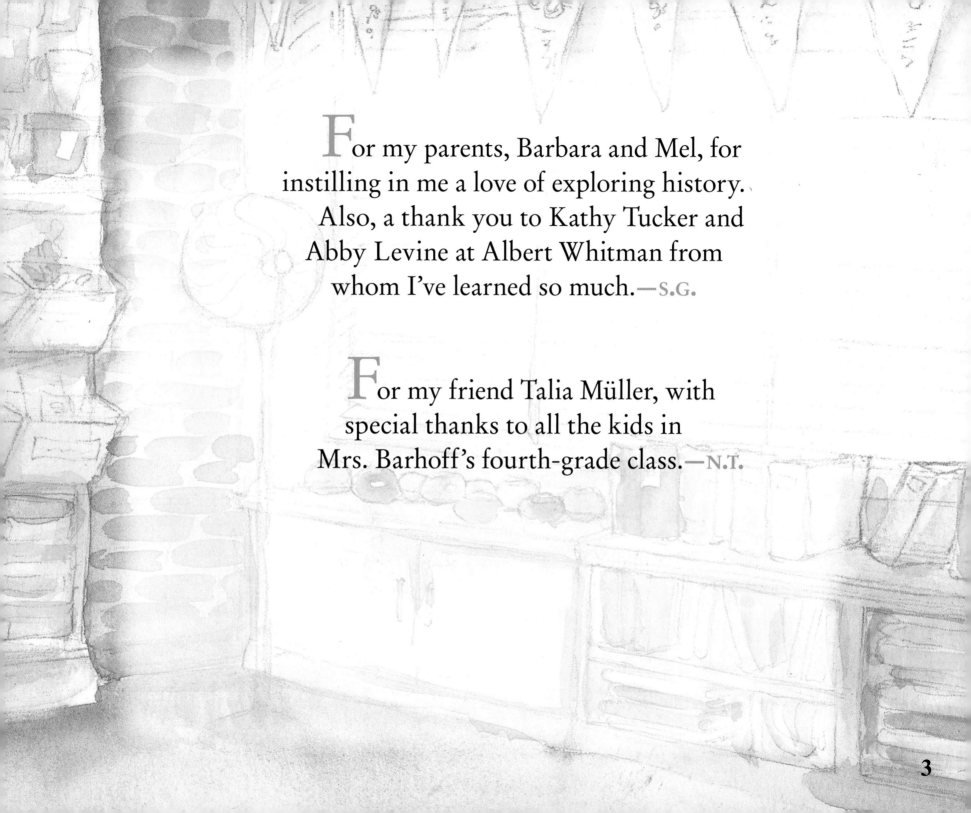

For my parents, Barbara and Mel, for instilling in me a love of exploring history. Also, a thank you to Kathy Tucker and Abby Levine at Albert Whitman from whom I've learned so much.—S.G.

For my friend Talia Müller, with special thanks to all the kids in Mrs. Barhoff's fourth-grade class.—N.T.

4

Every spring, Ms. Garcia's class grows a different kind of garden. In February, she announced that our class was going to plant a garden like Thomas Jefferson's.

"No fair," I whispered to my friend Shakayla. "Last year, they got to plant a pizza garden."

"Shhh," Shakayla replied as Ms. Garcia started saying something about a contest . . .

"A contest? What kind of contest?" I asked.

"A First Peas to the Table Contest, " Ms. Garcia said. "When Jefferson was older, he and his neighbors had one every spring. For our garden contest, you'll each be given a small spot for planting peas."

She held up a bowl. "The winner will be the first student who can fill this bowl with shelled peas and set them on the table to eat."

Some kids said "yuck," but Ms. Garcia said that fresh peas tasted as sweet as candy and were one of Jefferson's favorite foods.

"If peas taste as good as candy, I'm planting a ton," Shakayla said. "Let the great pea race begin!"

7

I really, *really* wanted to win when Ms. Garcia
showed us the winner's crown. It was green and
gold with emerald-colored pea-sized jewels all around it.
"Thomas Jefferson," she said, "called agriculture 'the crown' of
all the sciences."

"Be bold and experiment!" Ms. Garcia said.
"Jefferson traded seeds with people around the world.
Then he used his garden like a giant science lab to test
which plants would grow best."

I pulled a shiny nickel from my pocket. Jefferson was
on the front and his home, Monticello, was on the back.
This would be my good luck charm for winning, I decided.

The next day, we made journals to record our notes in, just like Thomas Jefferson did. His Garden Book was like a diary, with notes about everything he planted. And we learned a lot about peas.

Jefferson said that you had to have healthy soil to grow healthy plants. Compost, made of plant waste that's rotted, adds nutrients to the soil.

We took some compost from the school's bin and mixed it into the garden beds.

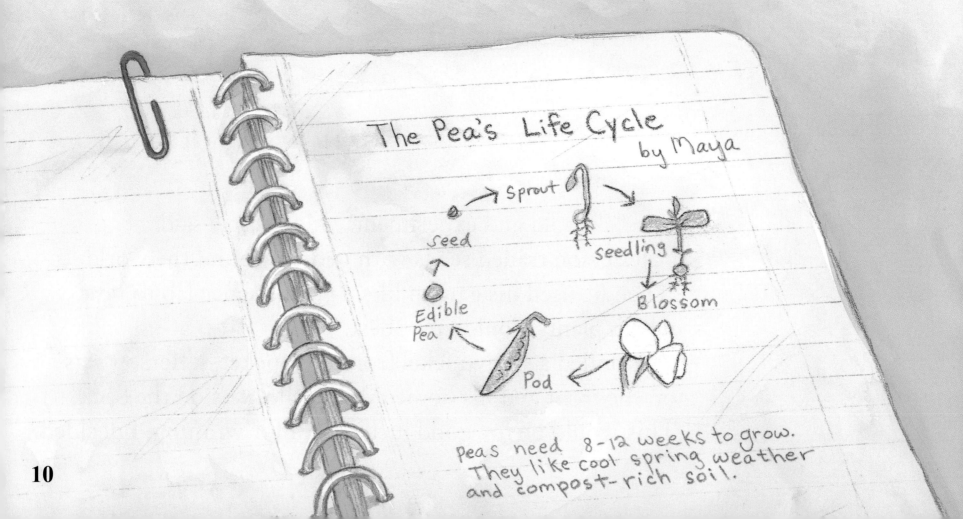

The Pea's Life Cycle by Maya

Sprout

seed

Edible Pea

seedling

Blossom

Pod

peas need 8-12 weeks to grow. They like cool spring weather and compost-rich soil.

On Valentine's Day, Ms. Garcia brought in ten different varieties of pea seeds. They had fancy names like "Emerald Treasures" and "Pearls in a Pod." We each got a packet of twenty seeds of one variety, and then we had a trading party.

Shakayla ended up with two seeds from each variety, but I held onto the twenty I started with—"Sweet Victory Peas." That name sounded like a winner to me.

Ms. Garcia said that we could get a head start by planting some peas inside at home and then transplanting them at school in March. But I was going to get a double head start because I'd found a pea-growing tip in a copy of Jefferson's Garden Book, and I was keeping it top secret . . .

At home, I put eight tiny pea seeds into a bowl of water.

"What are you doing?" my mother asked. "Making pea soup?"

"I'll tell you if you can keep it a secret," I told her. "In 1771, Jefferson wrote that he soaked his pea seeds for twenty-four hours before he planted them."

The next day, I planted my soaked seeds and placed the pots on a sunny windowsill with my good luck nickel next to them.

Four times a day, I checked on my plants and gave them water.

But after two weeks and no signs of green, I dug up a seed. It was rotten mush from too much water! So I started all over, with eight more seeds and less watering.

Maya's notes

Sweet Victory peas started indoors:

Planted	Up	1st Blossom	1st Pod	To Table
2/15				
3/1				

Shakayla started carrying home a lot of books on garden plants, and some strange stuff from the school's Recycling Resource Room.

"What's all this for?" I asked.

"Your peas aren't growing yet, are they?"

"Maybe," she smiled, "or maybe not. Are yours?"

"Maybe, or maybe not," I replied.

Shakayla laughed. "May the boldest gardener win!"

I ran home after school to check my peas.
My little seeds had started sprouting! I made
a name tag for each pot.

"Grow faster," I whispered to my plants.
"As soon as you're strong enough, I'm
moving you to a real garden."

On March twenty-first, the first day of spring, we worked on our garden's main beds. Like Jefferson, we divided them into three sections for roots, fruits, and leaves. But when we got ready to mark which plants went in which section, we got confused.

"Cucumbers and peppers aren't fruits," insisted Jacob. "They're vegetables." So Shakayla grabbed a science book and we sorted things out.

"Remember," Shakayla directed, "roots are foods that grow underground, like carrots. Leaves are leaves we eat, like lettuce. And cucumbers, peppers, and tomatoes are called fruits because they grow from a flower and have seeds inside the part that you eat. But those won't get planted until the weather warms up more."

The next day, I transplanted my eight home plants into my pea patch and I planted my last four seeds. Then I stuck in a whirligig to scare away the hungry birds. In the big garden bed, tiny ruffled lettuce leaves were coming up.

I felt like a gardening champion until I walked over to Shakayla's pea patch. It looked like a science fair exhibit! She had ten different types of peas, labeled like Jefferson's with numbers, and some of her transplants were twice the size of mine!

When I saw the different types of trellises she'd made, I remembered that peas like some kind of support. That way, they stay out of the mud and get more sunshine.

In April, we went outside every day to weed the beds and record the progress of our plants. Our lettuce was growing the fastest of all.

I invented a trellis for my peas with bells that played soft music in the wind. Jefferson won a gold medal for his invention of a garden plow. Maybe someday I'd win a gold medal for an invention, too.

One sunny day, I saw that Shakayla's plants had little white blossoms all over them. I raced to my pea patch, hoping to find some flowers on my plants.

Penelope Pea had a blossom! I was so happy that I did a little pea blossom dance.

Shakayla and I sat down and drew pea blossoms in our journals.

"I wish I could draw as well as you," she said.

"I wish that my plants were as big as yours," I replied.

"Thomas Jefferson almost always lost the First Peas to the Table Contest to his neighbor, Mr. Divers," Shakayla said, reminding me of the story Ms. Garcia had told us. "But they stayed friends."

"You're right," I said, giving her a hug. "But I still hope that my plants win."

By early May, I had lots of blossoms, and six blossoms had made tiny pods!

Maya's notes

Sweet Victory peas started indoors:

Planted	Up	1st Blossom	1st Pod	To Table
2/15 3/1	3/11	4/22	5/1	

4 seeds started outdoors:

Planted	Up	1st Blossom	1st Pod	To Table
3/22	4/3			

Only 3 of the 4 came up:
Perky, Peewee, and President

Pea blossoms and pods   5/3

One day the sky grew dark and a big windstorm came, hooting and hollering over the school. When it ended, we went outside to check our plants.

Mine were okay, but then I heard Shakayla crying out, "Oh, no!" Her trellises had tumbled into a terrible tangle.

"It looks like you'll win now," she said. "My plants are ruined."

"No, they're not," I said. "I'll help you fix them."

27

On the fourteenth of May, we had a celebration lunch with the first harvest of our lettuce and a bowl of fresh peas. But the peas were not mine.

They were Shakayla's, and she was crowned the winner of our First Peas to the Table Contest.

"Congratulations," I said. "You did a good job."

"Thanks," she said. "I bet that your plants will be second.

They look really good."

"Maybe," I replied. "But it feels like I've been waiting for them forever."

Then I went to check on my slowpoke peas.

My first pod, plump and firm, was ready to be picked! I plucked it off, popped it open, and tasted a pea. It *was* as sweet as candy. And I'd grown it all by myself.

No wonder Thomas Jefferson liked gardening so much—from one tiny seed, a whole plant could grow, full of flowers first, then giving you the sweetest peas in the whole world. Some things were worth waiting for.

Afterword

Thomas Jefferson (1743–1826) was the third president of the United States, author of the Declaration of Independence, an architect, inventor, and founder of the University of Virginia. But his most delightful work, he wrote in 1811, was to garden. His five-thousand-acre plantation at Monticello, his home in Virginia, included a thousand-foot-long vegetable garden. From 1766 to 1824, he recorded notes in a journal, called his Garden Book. In his neighborhood's contest, the winner served his peas at a dinner for the other gardeners.

Jefferson wanted Americans to use their land wisely, planting what grew best. So he sought out hundreds of new plants, experimented with them in his garden, and asked friends to do so, too. After doubling the size of the United States with the Louisiana Purchase in 1803, he asked Meriwether Lewis and William Clark to collect plants for him as they explored and mapped this territory. Jefferson believed that providing people with new plants that they could use was "the greatest service" that citizens could do for their country. He was especially proud of finding a rice that Americans could grow on dry land.

Jefferson called agriculture "the crown of all other sciences" as it required knowledge in many other sciences like botany and chemistry. He tested farming methods and invented an improved plow. Plowing deep and fertilizing the soil with manure, he wrote, were two keys to growing healthy plants. Those without animals, he noted, could use "vegetable manure" (compost). Although Jefferson and his family helped a little with the garden labor, it was the enslaved African-Americans and free workers who did most of the work on the large plantation. Jefferson promoted various antislavery laws, yet freed very few of the slaves at Monticello.

The restored gardens at Monticello can be visited today. First Lady Michelle Obama's White House Kitchen Garden also has a Thomas Jefferson section planted with some of his favorite foods like peas and tennis-ball lettuce. Vegetables were the main part of Jefferson's diet.